The
FIREBIRD

retold by ROBERT D. SAN SOUCI

pictures by KRIS WALDHERR

Dial Books for Young Readers

New York

To my very dear friend Audrey Berger
R.S.S.

❧ ☙

For Alan and Marja Lee
K.W.

Published by Dial Books for Young Readers
A Division of Penguin Books USA Inc.
375 Hudson Street
New York, New York 10014

Text copyright © 1992 by Robert D. San Souci
Pictures copyright © 1992 by Kris Waldherr
All rights reserved
Designed by Jane Byers Bierhorst
Printed in Hong Kong by
South China Printing Company (1988) Limited
First Edition
1 3 5 7 9 10 8 6 4 2

Library of Congress Cataloging in Publication Data

San Souci, Robert D.
The Firebird / by Robert D. San Souci
illustrated by Kris Waldherr
p. cm.
Summary / Prince Ivan wanders into an
enchanted garden and, with the help of the
magnificent Firebird, rescues a princess
from an evil sorcerer.
ISBN 0-8037-0799-1 (trade).—ISBN 0-8037-0800-9 (lib. bdg.)
[1. Folklore—Soviet Union. 2. Ballets—Stories, plots, etc.]
I. Waldherr, Kris, ill. II. Title.
PZ8.1.S227Fi 1992 398.2—dc20 [E] 91-574 CIP AC

The art for each picture consists of an oil painting
applied over a golden acrylic underpainting on
paper that had been stretched on a board,
gessoed, and sanded.

The illustrator would like to thank Amelia Lau Carling,
Dianne Clouet, Ellen Dreyer, Nilka Dunne,
Vincent Gottchalk, Dave Mazzeo, and Robert Olsson
for their help with this book.

L ong ago a prince named Ivan went hunting far from his own land. Deep in a dark wood he lost his way and began to fear he would never again see his home. He wandered, searching, until at last he discovered a high stone fence with a golden gate. Peering through the golden barrier, the young man saw a garden filled with graceful trees, jewellike flowers, and grass as fine as green silk.

Suddenly the garden blazed with a golden light. The young man watched the magnificent Firebird flitting from branch to branch. Her feathers were like streams of flame; her beak and claws, like burnished gold; her eyes sparkled like rubies. Sometimes it seemed a bird, sometimes a woman, that flickered through the leaves.

The Firebird lit on a tree laden with golden apples by the gate, and began preening her feathers. Ivan quickly climbed the stone wall. Close to the apple tree, he reached for the bow at his back. Then he stopped, not wanting to harm such a glorious creature.

From his belt he took a snare and flung the net over the Firebird. She cried out in anger. Then, to Ivan's shock, she said, "Your net binds me as no magic can. I will die in captivity. Free me, and I will give you a magic talisman that may save your life. This is a dangerous place—and much harder to escape than it seems."

As she spoke, the brilliant fire of her plumage faded; the tips of her wings turned ashen. Hastily Ivan removed the strands that trapped her.

Immediately she soared into the air, her feathers so radiant that the young man looked away for fear of being blinded.

Three times the bird circled above his head. The third time, she plucked a feather from her breast and dropped it down to the prince. It lay in Ivan's hands like a drop of molten gold.

"I give this to you in return for my freedom," the Firebird said. "If you need my help, wave it three times in the air, and I will come to you."

"Thank you," cried the prince, as the Firebird vanished into the depths of the vast garden. He folded the magic feather into his shirt, where he felt it resting warm against his heart.

Suddenly he heard playful shouts and saw a young woman dressed in violet, followed by other maidens, running across the lawn. Ivan stood entranced by the raven-haired beauty, whose pale cheeks grew red at his stare. The other young women whispered excitedly to one another, pointing at the prince.

At last Ivan said, "Lady, my name is Ivan, and I am at your service." He bowed to the woman, whose violet gown revealed her noble birth.

"I am the Princess Elena," she said. "These are my handmaidens.

"The wizard Kastchei, disguised as a black whirlwind, kidnapped us from my father's kingdom far away. Brave knights have tried to rescue us, but Kastchei turned them to stone." She pointed to statues of gallant knights standing amid the greenery.

Ivan clasped her pale hand. "Elena, let me help you escape."

Elena's dark eyes grew sad. "Anyone who enters this garden remains a prisoner. There is no escape. I've tried many times."

"Even if the gate is locked," Ivan protested, "we can climb the wall."

"Poor Ivan, look again," said Elena.

Turning, Ivan found that the wall now reached up to the clouds, and the gate had disappeared. But the warmth of the Firebird's feather folded into his breast gave him courage. "I have a magic talisman that will help us," he said. "Now tell me about this wizard."

"Kastchei is powerful and cunning," she responded. "No one can escape his garden while he lives. But he is called The Deathless One, because no one knows where his death is hidden."

"Where is he now?" Ivan wondered.

"Away on some mysterious errands," she said.

Ivan, anxious to impress the beautiful young woman, said boldly, "When he returns, I will use my magic talisman to free us all."

The Princess Elena, who had herself fallen in love with Ivan, took hope. She ordered her servants to spread damask cloths on the lawn. They offered Ivan baked meats on bronze platters, wheaten loaves on silver trays, and green wine in crystal goblets. Afterward they played catch with golden apples and silver pears, and as the day waned, they sang songs and told riddles.

Ivan, who was basking in Elena's bright glances, had never known such happiness.

Abruptly the skies grew dark, and violet lightning flashed above the garden.

"Kastchei is returning," said Elena, drawing Ivan close while the other women huddled together.

The air around them began to hum. Then the humming grew to a howling that split the sky. A dark storm cloud descended to the garden and changed into a tall, slender figure in swirling black robes. Just as the Firebird had appeared to Ivan sometimes a bird, sometimes a woman, so the magician appeared as sometimes a man, sometimes a skeleton with black bones and eyes of chilling black fire.

When Kastchei saw the prince he cried, "What an unexpected pleasure! I am always delighted to greet visitors. Let us clasp hands in friendship."

But Elena held Ivan back saying, "His touch will turn you to stone!"

With a harsh laugh the magician raised his arms. Hideous ogres and trolls and other monsters tumbled from the sleeves of his robe and crept from beneath its hem. They menaced Ivan on every side, so filling him with horror that he could think of nothing else. He bravely drew his sword, but the creatures darted at him and danced away from his blade, mocking his efforts.

Suddenly Elena, remembering what Ivan had told her, cried out, "Use your talisman to save yourself!"

The young man drew out the Fire-bird's feather and waved it in the air one, two, three times.

Instantly the garden was bathed in a golden glow as the creature with plumes of flame blazed like a comet through the air to protect Ivan inside the circle of her golden light.

Blinded, the monsters stumbled over one another, then quickly fell into a deep sleep.

"Now, Ivan!" called the Firebird. "I can only delay Kastchei a few more moments. In his garden you will find a green-wooded oak beside a well. At its root is a copper key. This will un-lock the secret of Kastchei's death that is hidden in his palace."

"I know the very tree," Elena said. She led Ivan to the massive oak. At its root they found the copper key, just as the Firebird had promised. On it was inscribed:

I open the casket in the copper room
That draws Kastchei closer to his doom.

Before they left, Elena filled a pitcher from the well beside the tree, saying, "This water, sprinkled on any living creature, will put it to sleep."

Then she guided Ivan to a palace of white stone with a golden roof. There a three-headed dragon was guarding a copper door. It hissed and spat fire, but Elena sprinkled it with water from the well, and it promptly fell asleep.

Inside was a room of beaten copper. Ivan and Elena found the copper casket, and Ivan used the copper key to open it. Inside was a tiny silver key. On this was written:

I open the casket in the silver room
That draws Kastchei closer to his doom.

Together the prince and princess now hurried down a passageway of white stone to a door of silver, guarded by a six-headed dragon.

Again Elena sprinkled the monster with the magic water, but the power had grown weaker. It was a long time before the dragon's heads drooped, one by one, into slumber.

They entered a chamber walled in silver. Unlocking the silver casket they found there, they discovered a golden key. It bore the legend:

I open the casket in the golden room
That hides the secret of Kastchei's doom.

A final corridor brought them to a roaring twelve-headed dragon, barring a golden door. The magic water Elena sprinkled on the dragon's scales boiled away harmlessly. Ivan dipped the Firebird's feather into the nearly empty pitcher, then flung the last few drops over the dragon. In a trice the monster crashed to the floor, asleep.

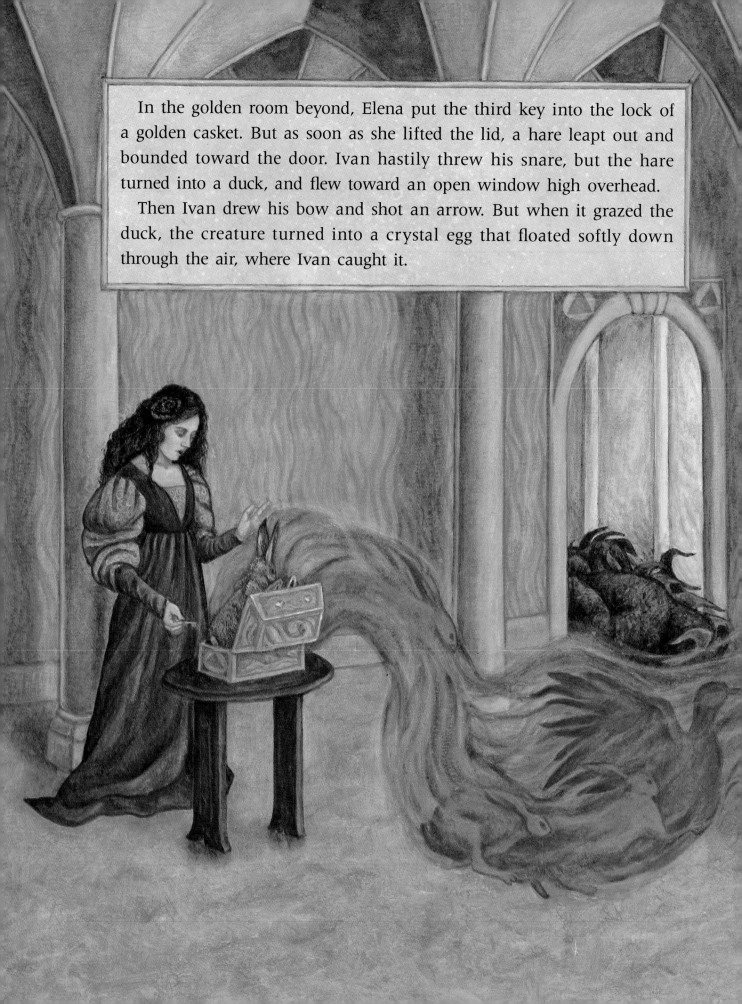

In the golden room beyond, Elena put the third key into the lock of a golden casket. But as soon as she lifted the lid, a hare leapt out and bounded toward the door. Ivan hastily threw his snare, but the hare turned into a duck, and flew toward an open window high overhead.

Then Ivan drew his bow and shot an arrow. But when it grazed the duck, the creature turned into a crystal egg that floated softly down through the air, where Ivan caught it.

At that instant the Firebird flew into the room, followed by Kastchei.

When Kastchei saw Ivan holding the crystal egg he said, "Give me that bauble, and I will give you your freedom and wealth beyond measure."

"Do not listen to him!" warned the Firebird. "That crystal holds his life."

Hearing these words the wizard changed himself into a raging whirlwind, with a frightening black shape like a skeleton at its heart. The chamber crackled with his terrible power.

But Ivan threw the crystal egg to the floor, shattering it in a blaze of black fire. Instantly the howling winds died away to silence. The skeletal shape crumbled into ashes. Kastchei the Deathless was no more.

When Ivan, Elena, and the Firebird returned to the garden, they found the knights who had been turned to statues freed from the evil wizard's spell. The stone wall around the garden was gone; the wizard's monsters had returned to their original shapes—frogs and beetles, mice and lizards—and fled to the forest.

Ivan and Elena thanked the Firebird for all she had done. She, in turn, wished them happiness and promised to come to them if they ever needed her help. As the couple embraced, the radiant creature flew away toward the east, until the fire of her plumes and the fire of the rising sun seemed one in the same.

The prince and princess returned to Ivan's kingdom, accompanied by the restored knights and the rescued maidens.

They were married in the great hall, hung with tapestries emblazoned with images of the Firebird. From that time forward the kingdom's banners always pictured the Firebird.

Ivan and Elena ruled so wisely that they never had to call upon the Firebird again. But her golden feather, in a crystal casket, remained their dearest possession.